Cinderella

Retold by Ian Robinson
Illustrated by Gerry Embleton

ap
award publications limited

Printed in Belgium

ISBN 0 86163 006 8
© Award Publications Ltd. 1980
Spring House, Spring Place,
London NW5, England

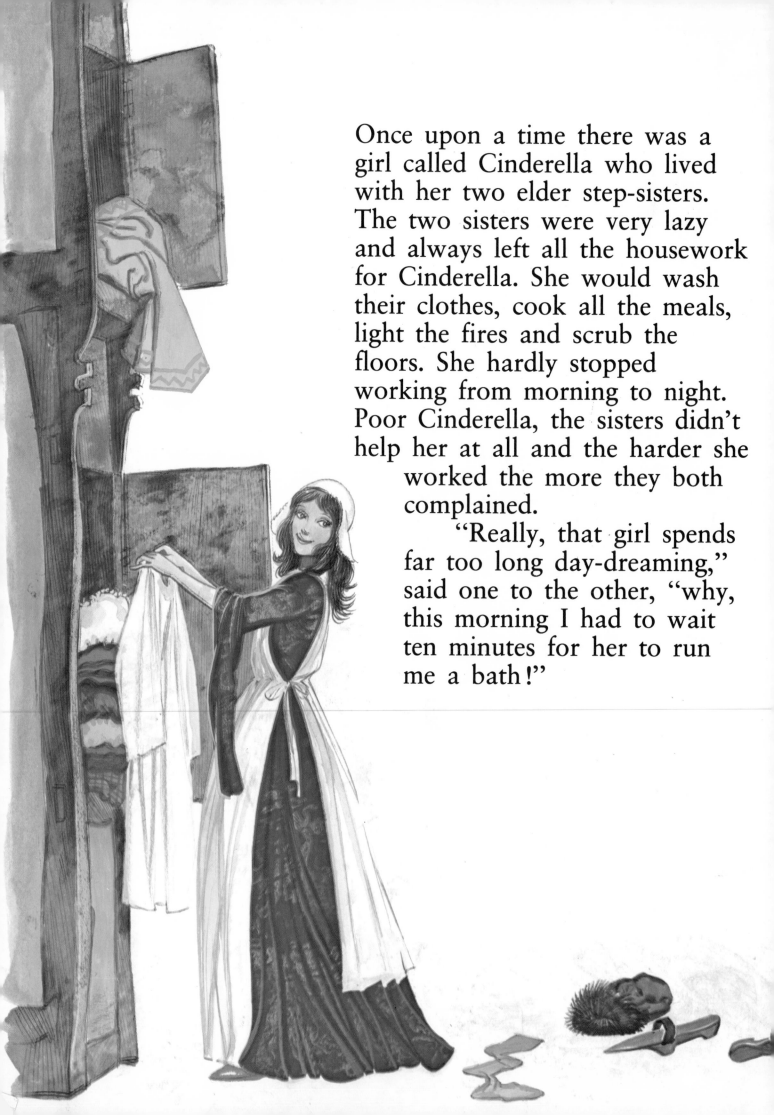

Once upon a time there was a girl called Cinderella who lived with her two elder step-sisters. The two sisters were very lazy and always left all the housework for Cinderella. She would wash their clothes, cook all the meals, light the fires and scrub the floors. She hardly stopped working from morning to night. Poor Cinderella, the sisters didn't help her at all and the harder she worked the more they both complained.

"Really, that girl spends far too long day-dreaming," said one to the other, "why, this morning I had to wait ten minutes for her to run me a bath!"

Cinderella never complained, everyday she did whatever the sisters asked and had hardly a moment to spare. While her ugly sisters spent hours choosing fine, new dresses and arranging their hair, Cinderella wore rags and went barefoot, for they never gave her any money to spend on herself. She even slept huddled close to the fire, down among the cinders.

One day a messenger called at the house with a letter addressed to them all. The Prince was holding a Grand Ball and all three sisters were invited to come and join in the dancing.

It was to last for two whole nights and invitations had gone out all over the kingdom.

"How delightful!" said the sisters, "All the most handsome young men in the kingdom will be there, we must be sure to look our best."

"And I can come too!" Cinderella cried excitedly.

"Don't be ridiculous child!" the sisters snapped, "You can't go anywhere looking like a ragged little servant-girl, and besides, we'll need you here to help us get ready in time."

Without a moment's delay, the sisters went out to buy some new shoes for the evening. "Let's have no more nonsense about you coming to the Ball too," they told Cinderella as they left, "make sure you have everything done by the time we come home."

As she laid out her sisters fine dresses and helped them to get ready, Cinderella's lip trembled and tears trickled down her nose. Her sisters didn't even notice as they swept grandly into the carriage. Back by the fireside, Cinderella sobbed, "It's not fair! Why should they have all the fun? I was invited to the Ball too, it said so in the letter."
At her words a brilliant light filled the room and to her astonishment, a kindly old lady appeared.

"I am your fairy godmother, Cinderella. Dry your eyes my dear," she said, "you shall go to the Ball this evening whatever your selfish, ugly sisters say!"

Cinderella was overjoyed and hugged the kind old lady. "That would be wonderful," she cried, "but how can I go to the Ball dressed in these old rags, I've got nothing to wear at all."

The old lady explained that she would make a spell to help Cinderella on her way, all they needed were a few things from the garden.

First she told Cinderella to cut the largest pumpkin she could find and then she sent her into the kitchen to bring out the mouse trap. Inside were six white mice and a fat, black rat. "They will be perfect," chuckled her godmother, "now bring me six newts from the river and our spell will be almost complete."

When, at last, Cinderella had gathered this strange collection together the old woman stood them all in the moonlight and waved her magic wand. "Her journey at the palace ends, come speed her carriage my fine friends." she said. To Cinderella's astonishment a magnificent carriage and a team of six white horses stood where she had put the mice and the pumpkin.

The old woman smiled happily, then turned to the
rat and the six newts. "In costume fine these
grooms shall ride with Cinderella safe inside."
Just as before, the newts and the rat were gone.
In their place stood six tall grooms and a jolly
coachman, all dressed in fine livery waiting to
take Cinderella to the palace in her splendid
coach.

All that Cinderella needed now was something to wear to the Ball instead of her everyday rags. Her fairy godmother told her to close her eyes and count to ten while she cast another spell.

"In these fine robes a Princess rides to make the Prince a perfect bride."

When Cinderella opened her eyes she found herself dressed in the most beautiful silk gown and dainty glass slippers.

"Hurry now child," the old woman called as Cinderella climbed into the awaiting carriage, "you can dance all evening, but remember, you must leave the Ball before twelve o'clock for then the magic ends and all your fine clothes will turn to rags once more."

Soon Cinderella was speeding through the night as her six white horses galloped like the wind. At last they came to the castle where the gates were wide open and light shone from every window. In the distance Cinderella could hear music playing and people talking excitedly, the Ball was just about to start.

At first Cinderella was a little nervous of all the finery she found inside the castle, but soon she was enjoying the dancing along with everyone else. Up and down the dancers went, round and round they swirled. Cinderella found herself dancing with a handsome young man who kissed her hand when the music stopped. Everyone was envious, especially her two ugly sisters, for it was the Prince himself who had chosen her as his partner. "This girl is the most beautiful I have seen in the whole kingdom," he thought to himself, "I do hope she comes again tomorrow."

Although she would have liked to stay longer, Cinderella remembered her god-mother's warning and was home before the bells rang out for mid-night. She was already back in her rags when the sisters came home and she pretended to have spent the evening sitting by the fireside, waiting for their return.

"What a lovely evening," they declared, "it was simply wonderful, although the Prince spent the whole evening dancing with some beautiful girl!" Cinderella didn't say anything, she just smiled, the sisters had not recognised her at all.

On the second evening of the Ball,
Cinderella rode to the castle in her
carriage again, making sure that her
sisters thought she was all alone at
home. The Prince was delighted to
see her again and partnered her in
every dance. As the evening wore
on they began to fall in love.

"I must have this girl as my bride," thought the Prince as he looked into her beautiful, clear blue eyes.
Cinderella was so happy, she forgot all about her god-mother's warning and was still dancing with the Prince as the clock began to strike twelve. "Goodness me!" she cried and ran out of the castle into the darkness before anyone saw her dressed in rags like a little servant-girl.

The Prince ran after Cinderella but she was hidden in the shadows before he could see which direction she had taken.

"Search the grounds!" he called to the palace guard, "that girl must be found. Search the grounds everyone — at once!"
But although the Prince and his soldiers searched high and low for Cinderella all that he found was one of her little glass slippers. It had fallen from her foot as she ran down the steps into the garden. "I will find the girl who wore this slipper," the Prince declared, "And when next she comes to the palace she will come here as my bride."

Early the next morning, an order
went out that every girl in the
kingdom was to try on the glass
slipper, for whoever it fitted
would marry the Prince.

People came from far and wide, the beautiful and
the ugly, the tall and the short, the slender and the
stout. Not one of them could wear the little slipper.

"Try again tomorrow!" said the Prince when the
news was brought to him by a messenger,
"somewhere in the kingdom my beautiful partner
must be found."

Eventually the soldiers brought the slipper to Cinderella's house where her sisters rushed to try it on. How they pushed and pulled trying to make the slipper fit, but they had no more luck than anyone else, the slipper could not possibly belong to either of them.

"Does anyone else live here?" the soldiers asked when the sisters had given up their struggle. "All must try the slipper."

"Only Cinderella!" laughed the sisters, "but the Prince can't marry a servant-girl."

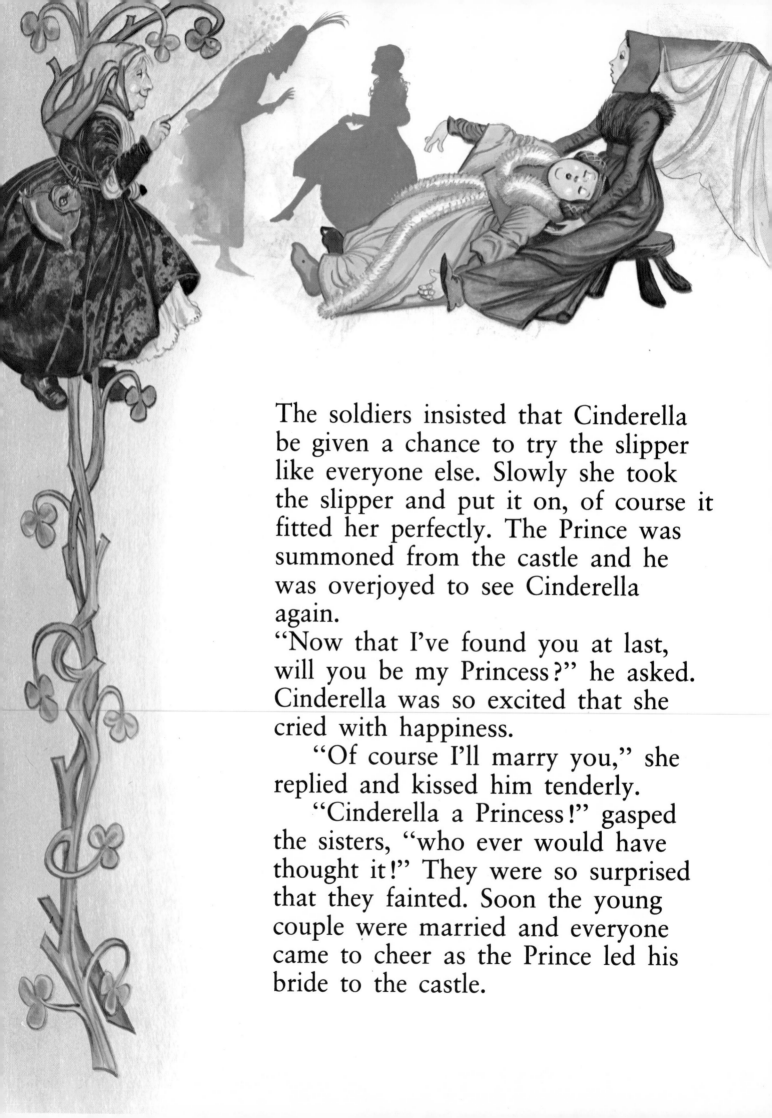

The soldiers insisted that Cinderella
be given a chance to try the slipper
like everyone else. Slowly she took
the slipper and put it on, of course it
fitted her perfectly. The Prince was
summoned from the castle and he
was overjoyed to see Cinderella
again.

"Now that I've found you at last,
will you be my Princess?" he asked.
Cinderella was so excited that she
cried with happiness.

"Of course I'll marry you," she
replied and kissed him tenderly.

"Cinderella a Princess!" gasped
the sisters, "who ever would have
thought it!" They were so surprised
that they fainted. Soon the young
couple were married and everyone
came to cheer as the Prince led his
bride to the castle.

The years passed and eventually Cinderella and the Prince became King and Queen of the whole kingdom. Their reign was happy and peaceful and they were loved by all their subjects. Even the ugly sisters rejoiced at their sisters good fortune, when they had recovered from their surprise and were never cruel or hateful to her again.